OLIVE TREES IN

BY

TANYA WHITE

For Rosa and Dougie

"No man is an island"

(John Donne)

Acknowledgements

My thanks to my dear friend, Dr Seda Boghossian-Tighe, MBChB, MSc, PhD, MRCPath(1), DFFP, DID, whose work and endless compassion have proved inspirational.

Biography

Tanya White is a human rights barrister, practising from Ventnor. She is the acclaimed author of two previous books, 'The Thirty-Year Night' and 'Re-Setting the World'.

She has three children and two grandchildren, and now lives on the Isle of Wight with her husband and their Old English Sheepdog, Basil.

From the author of 'The Thirty-Year Night' and 'Re-Setting the World' comes the paradox of migration. An environmental trilogy. Much of the earth has become uninhabitable, as global warming passes Level 3 tipping. Mass migration begins to the far North.

What happens when we become the refugees? Through the eyes of one United Kingdom family and their friends leaving a dying country, we meet a smorgasbord of emotions, seasoned with conflicting acts of love and hate, greed and generosity, terror and calmness, manifesting in crime, compassion, disinformation, honesty, order and disobedience. Wrapped in dark humour and farce, the ultimate truth will unfold.

OLIVE TREES IN NORWAY

by

TANYA WHITE

Chapter 1.

THE BOMBSHELL

The leaves on the olive trees were starting to wither, the vine was trying to flourish with a dearth of water and the bees ambled rather than swarmed around the honeysuckle as the birds stayed silent. Down the hill the sun sparkled on the blue-green sea, as the heat rose violently, time outside would be limited. Bernard, a Newfoundland, formerly trained as a rescue dog but now of retirement age, lay stretched out on the grass, guarding the Ramsay family, and eyeing scraps as they tucked into fresh eggs and warm bread – all except the eldest daughter. "Olivia, can't you stop looking at that contraption, at least while we're eating?" Her silence slightly angered her father, Jeremy. He glanced at his wife, Maria, but it was her younger brother, Nicholas, who picked up the baton. "I haven't brought my mobile to the table, so why should you be able to use yours? It's not fair." Still silence. Family tension rose with the heat.

Olivia looked at her family, tears in her eyes. "What's wrong? Has Michael been playing around with other girls again? I told you..." Olivia interrupted her mother Maria "What was the point of everything, what use are those exams I've just passed? I could have spent more time with the boy I love, why didn't you let me stay with him? I hated that holiday job...". She returned her focus to the mobile, this time without family recrimination...eating stopped...alerts were read...silence reigned. Bernard had significantly more than just scraps.

Jeremy showed disbelief. "It must be fake news. It can't be right. It's ridiculous! You cannot just have a whole lot of European countries, from Portugal and Spain to Bulgaria, Greece and Cyprus, just suddenly burning up, killing millions. Or other countries like Bangladesh or Indonesia being not just flooded but totally submerged, with their populations. It's just not possible! Anyway, world governments had finally agreed to implement global carbon quotas." He didn't appreciate that the stable door had by now closed and the horses had bolted.

At that moment there was a knock on the door. It was Dr Samera Quresh. "Maria, is this true? I don't understand. Is this fake? My understanding was that the world consortium were going to implement carbon quotas in good time to avert this?" She had left Bangladesh to work in the NHS and was renting the house next door, with her brother, Dr Anjum Karim. Their families should have joined them by now, but the Home Office was overwhelmed with work and had fallen behind with processing their applications.

Olivia came rushing to the door. "There's going to be an address to the nation in 30 minutes...I feel sick." Maria and Jeremy feigned calm whilst their blood pressure rose. Samera and Anjum had fortified themselves with valium, but Olivia and Nicholas picked up bloodcurdling vibes...the shock, fear and stress would manifest physically in the young adults. Anjum fetched his medical bag.

11am, Thursday 5th June 2030. BBC World News.

This is your Prime Minister speaking. I must ask you to brace yourselves for some terrible news. On screen you will see a list of countries which have been burnt or flooded. There have been billions of deaths. This is a disaster on a biblical scale. The Government has scientific data now confirming that "tipping stage 3" has abruptly begun.

Time is of the essence. I have enlisted the army to deliver emergency packages to collection points throughout the country. You will receive a text detailing where to collect your package. I have a curfew in various towns and cities, at set times. The reason for this will shortly be apparent.

The fires in Southern Europe are gaining in heat, speed and momentum. I am therefore organizing the evacuation of this country towards the North. Countries in the Eastern Bloc are taking similar action, migrating from Russia and countries in south-eastern Europe towards the Arctic coast and Siberia, while the people of the United States are moving to Canada.

(He did not tell them the Russian Federation was trying to block migration from China and Japan to Eastern Siberia and preventing passage northwards from the countries on its southern border. Nor did he explain that the Canadian Government had agreed to admit only one quarter of the US population.)

The passage will be by sea. The Army will be issuing your passes, and guiding groups to collection points. You will all understand that the younger generations must have priority. The Army has orders to shoot those who try to prevent the fair, just and orderly evacuation of the people. You are all aware of my mandate, to safeguard human rights above all else. It is a paradox, but I have to balance the rights of the young, who have barely lived, and who have played no part in bringing about this carnage, against the rights of the older generations. My scales have weighed in the rights of younger generations as paramount

There will be limited space in the ships. Pocket possessions and Government issue food parcels only will be permitted, anything else will be confiscated.

For those who do not wish to evacuate, the Government will issue appropriate medication for a pain-free and quick suicide.

I will take questions now from the press, but only a few, there is much to be done."

"Francis Philby, Reuters…When people tried to migrate here, we turned them away. What guarantee do you have that the Nordic countries can or will accommodate us?"

This was a tough one. The PM, James Cuthbertson, had just given the nation catastrophic news and unimaginably harsh demands. How could he also tell them that the Nordic countries didn't want them. They would allow only a pitiful percentage of the European countries. Oh, he had begged and pleaded, threatened them, including with hellfire in the hereafter, but…There was no choice but to turn up en masse. The Nordic countries could hardly then send them back. Even if they had the means, that would amount to genocide. No, he had made up his mind, he would have to lie or kill what little hope they had, and the latter course would be like a death knell.

"We are currently in negotiation with our Nordic friends, and the British Government is confident of a fruitful outcome. For some time now, the Nordic climate has mirrored the old Mediterranean countries, they have planted in fertile soils yielding phenomenal crops. Indications show great compassion towards our refugee status."

"Geoffrey Holding, the Guardian...Prime Minister, we have known about the perils of global warming for over 50 years. The World Science Consortium, Quantum, has been screaming for carbon quotas. Why was nothing done?"

"We are in a state of emergency, Geoffrey. Now is not the time for whys and wherefores of the past. Please keep your questions to the here and now."

"James Fox, the London Herald...How are you going to marshal millions of people and get them onto ships? And are there in any case enough ships?"

"The army has full instructions. The system of passes addresses that issue. We have a large fleet of naval and merchant vessels, and in addition the United Kingdom Maritime Association is requisitioning every seaworthy boat, barge, ship, cruiser and yacht in the country."

"Emily Jones, the Independent...How long has the government known that the world had passed the 3rd tipping point?"

The PM paused. For several years the governments had been put on notice that "tipping 3" could occur at any time, in full knowledge that stage 4 would render all life extinct and that it was dependent on surges in energy use worldwide. Whilst countries were at war and ever-increasing armouries were despatched, coal was burned, against protocol, to meet immediate needs. It all created a ticking bomb. This knowledge was sealed in a box to be hidden in the deepest recesses of the mind, while simultaneously wearing a comfort blanket – "science will come up with something", "everyone's doing their bit", "it's probably all exaggerated". He held on to this thought while speaking, answering the question from a different dimension.

"Whilst the Government took the precaution of preparing for a worst-case scenario, rather like we built numerous nuclear shelters during the potential crisis with the East, we were not aware of the imminence or impact of the tipping point. We are all aware now, so let me go back to urgent preparations to ensure the safety of our people. As I said to Geoffrey, now is not the time for recriminations but for action. Thank you."

Jeremy comforted his family, speaking calmly but firmly. "We are going to get through this. There is refuge and everything is organized. I've just had a text regarding our emergency package. Before I leave, there are things you need to do. Maria, can you phone my brother, Mike, his family is living with Grandpa Morris?"

"Yes, of course. I'll phone my sister as well and see if it's all right down there with Mum."

"Olivia, can you make sure all mobiles are fully charged and get the cash from the safe place, and Nicholas, go through the camping clothing and sort out things with zip pockets and waterproofs, the best quality ones."

He then set out in detail a number of further requests, of no consequence in themselves but intended to keep his family focussed and busy.

"Hello Mike, it's Maria." She paused, words couldn't express the fear which was engulfing her, body and soul, a fear which she had to mask in front of her children. Small talk was impossible. Mike picked this up. "We have our emergency package, we're just waiting on our travel text. There's a problem though. The kids are devoted to Grandpa Morris, we all are, he's done so much for us. He's not a man of means himself but he got us out of bankruptcy, paid the school fees, gave us emotional support…you name it. But he's insisting he won't come, won't take room when someone younger could go without. He says he'll slow us down."

"Mike, he probably won't get a pass anyway."

"That's very much the problem. The kids won't leave him. They've been brought up in a world of plenty, everything on tap, grandparents living long lives, freely enjoying loving attachments, emphasis on the importance of every individual life. Now, trying to shift their mindset to stoical survival mode is like shifting the Forth Bridge. "

The conversation ended as it started, with terrifying thoughts, unspoken but very much understood.

The days passed. No travel passes arrived. Grandpa Morris had time to contact his lifelong friends Robert and Melissa. They all had similar interests and were the same vintage – they all used to be barristers in chambers together, specialising in human rights law.

"Morris, we'll be around about 9 tonight. We'll watch the sunset together in our special place. Remember when your Monica was alive, we four had a ball! All those midnight swims…"

That evening, Mike answered the door and saw them all out, saying "Have a good evening, guys." Morris, Robert and Melissa drove to the top of St Boniface Down.

"Here you are" said Rob "one bottle of Napoleon brandy."

"Thank you, Rob. Look, there's the sun in all its glory setting over the sea and darkening the land. It feels so much that we are part of the cosmos, all atoms linked together."

"We are just water and bacteria, physically, and so we go back to the earth, leaving behind only our thoughts and actions. I think, Morris, that we've lived honest lives, and helped a fair few people along the way. Don't you agree, Melissa?"

She nodded. "Look, Morris, now the sun has set, look at the stars. There's Orion and Cassiopeia, and behind us Ursa Major and Ursa Minor."

They marvelled at the beauty of the night sky, wrapped themselves in love, framed their old memories and took their government-issue pills with the last of the brandy, slipping quietly away, at peace with themselves and the world.

"Viv, how long did Grandpa say he'd be?"

"He didn't, but he'll probably be back later."

Soon, however, they were fretting. On checking his room Viv found a note.

"I have had the most wonderful life. 40 years with my soul mate, 2 children who have given me such pride in their compassionate and honourable natures, grandchildren, nieces and nephews whom I adore, a career I loved and deep and genuine friendships. I have found great solace in living an honourable life, and to detract from that now would cause me great sorrow, such that I would find living undignified and humiliating. The spaces in the ships are precious. Priority must be, and for once I agree with the Government, for the younger generations who have yet to live their lives. Many of my generation fear that their legacy will be that we usurped the world's resources. Please allow us at least to try to mitigate that catastrophic damage. The greatest thing you can do for me is to live, and fight on. I am with you in your hearts and minds. Later, grieve if you must, but for now you do not have the time for the luxury of grieving.

With all my love,

Grandpa"

But they did grieve. The eldest child wailed for what seemed like hours while the younger withdrew into himself. Mike felt as if his life's anchor had gone. Viv had already lost her own father, and now she had lost the man she loved as much. But her duty was to hold the family together. The passes could arrive at any time.

Chapter 2.

MISSING

"Jeremy, I think I can cope, it's like I have undergone some kind of metamorphosis. Gone into auto pilot, sunk all emotion, just want to get our kids on a ship."

"It's all you can do now darling, best place. Better phone your sister though if you are still worried."

"Hi Emily, it's Maria. How are you coping?"

"I don't know what to do Maria. You know how difficult Mum's been, she wants me to stay with her, thinks it will all be fine"

"I didn't think she had dementia."

"She hasn't. She knows the reality, but you know Mum, she's able to believe and get what she wants. Right now, it's me looking after her until hell freezes over."

"You have to go."

"I don't know, Mum's probably right, I'm no use to anyone, might as well keep her happy."

"For heaven's sake Emily, the country is crying out for help, children in care need accompanying to ships and there isn't enough manpower, distribution centres are in urgent need, the list is endless...you can make a difference...you cannot help Mum".

"Dad?"

"What is it, Nicholas?"

"I was laying out the utility clothing and I wanted Olivia to check which ones she wanted...fussy and all that...but I can't find her. Last time I saw her she was talking to Michael. She's kept his address secret."

The family searched the house, the neighbourhood, everywhere. They called the police but got no joy. If only they had realised that he was local.

Michael's Mum was in a state of anxiety, packing and unpacking, when she opened the door to Olivia. "What are you doing here, you should be at home waiting for your passes."

"I must see Michael...please."

"He's gone to Blake Street Town Hall to collect our passes, we leave soon. I don't know how long we will have a decent network connection, or whether it will cope with high seas and burning heat, but it's fine for now, you can call him and wait here...do your parents know where you are...come back!"

Olivia ran off impetuously towards Blake Street, frightened, excited, panicking, happy, terrified. Teenage hormones subjected to a world catastrophe which had dropped without warning had turned toxic, a once rational, intelligent young woman had morphed into a thunderbolt in a sea of emotion.

Maria was desperate and Jeremy was having difficulty feigning calm.

"Hello? This is the third time I've called this station. It is urgent. Calls to my daughter's phone are consistently unanswered. She's never disappeared before. Please can you help us find her?"

"I am sorry Mrs Ramsay. There is no-one here but me and I'm just the receptionist. You must realize, with the state of emergency all the police are assisting the army in trying to organize the evacuation of millions. Our instructions are strict and from on high."

"Are you telling me here's no active police force anywhere available to investigate crime?"

"They have to maintain order here and now, Mrs Ramsay."

"So paedophiles, murderers, rapists can all run amok?"

"Jeremy, that bloody woman has just hung up on me!"

"Leave that Maria, Bernard's trained in search and rescue."

I'll get some of Olivia's clothes with her scent."

"I can't hold him Dad, he's pulling my arm off."

"You're right. And it's not like him to be so manic. I've heard rumblings about dogs having a sixth sense...the old boy's devoted to Olivia...we'll just follow him."

"Jeremy, Nicholas, you run on. I'm slowing you down. I'll go back."

"OK, Olivia might turn up at home anyway. "

Olivia had finally reached the Town Hall, eagerly she scanned the long queue...she clocked the back of a young man, resembled Mike, but it couldn't be..he had his arm around a rather beautiful young woman...she stalked them like a leopard...it was him, she turned and ran...faster and faster until tripping and falling roadside, the car didn't stop, passers by didn't stop...was everyone on autopilot? All emotion buried?

"Dad, that's her...Bernard's found her"

"Stand back, Nicholas, I'll have to carry her, she's dazed and injured. "

Chapter 3.

THE DOCTORS

"Samira, you have to accept that they are gone. The Amnesty International report has been verified. The flooding in Bangladesh was on a truly biblical scale."

"No, no, all that chaos, they cannot be sure. My boys and husband are resilient, they would have found a way, I just know, we need to get back."

"The internet is working now, read this and look at the geographical report. Our country has been flooding for years, it's under now...all of it. Going back? Impossible, never mind a lack of transport, you'd have to wade through fire and water. You're in denial, Samera'

Samera fell to the floor, on her knees, it would have been less painful if her very heart had been ripped out. She hated herself, this metamorphosed into anger directed at Anjum;

"You've been drinking again."

"What do you expect? Facing reality was hard, you know how much I loved my wife and kids, and it's worse, Romana begged me to stay, she said the visas for the family might never arrive. I would give anything to have died with them, I'm a shell now, a little guilt swishing about an otherwise barren soul." He opened another bottle. Samira joined him.

"If the visas hadn't been delayed, they would have been with us now. Why did they take so long Anjum?"

"The old 'funding' chestnut. Though they had enough funds to send officials over to entice us medics to come to the UK and fill the shortages, promising fast-paced family visas, and the earth, excuse the pun. If only we had chased up the visas, or if… We messed up Samera, we caused their fate, if we…'

"Look, Anjum, you can go over and over the past, all the 'what if, what if not?' questions. If our families' visas had come through on time, we'd be together. If the true state of global warming hadn't been hushed up…If we hadn't studied medicine…no, Anjum, recriminations make no sense. I doubt we'd even get passes anyway without having settled status, and that's 3 years off now, even if we did, what's the point? I can't live with this burdening grief, and you'll be dead soon of liver failure the rate you're knocking it back."

As they began rummaging around for the Government pills there was a loud bang on the door. Death would have to wait a little.

"Please help us. It's Olivia. She's drowsy, she can't stand up." Instead of rummaging for suicide pills Samira and Anjum started rummaging for equipment and medicines and examining Olivia.

"She's very cold Anjum, I'll hold her close while you examine her...what are her vitals?"

"She's physically fine, but clearly suffering from extreme stress and shock...warm blankets, hot soup, some tranquilisers, I'll get on with it."

For some hours, they sat with Olivia, updating Maria at regular intervals, having persuaded her to allow them space. Finally, there was the most soul destroying cry, as if Olivia was releasing a demon comprised of terror, fear and sorrow...then, endless flowing tears. Anjum tried to lift her spirits, armed with love, compassion, and strong anti-depressant medication (personally he preferred the bottle, natural grape juice he called it, but.) For Olivia, losing Mike in such cruel circumstances was the straw that broke the camel's back. "No one, let alone youngsters, is able to mentally process and accept what is happening. Coming from a society that counsels counselling if you happen to glance at a 'pub punch up' just compounds the difficulty. So, for now Olivia, don't try to process anything, just go through the motions of what needs to be done daily, in preparation for your evacuation. Try to find little gentle pleasures, like stroking Bernard, hugging your parents and brother. Don't dwell on the past or guess at the future, let hope in."

Mention of Bernard touched a chord, two in fact, one of love and another of concern, as she vaguely recollected him limping.

"Samira, I'm exhausted. But glad we were able to help. Would you like me to cook a little celebratory meal? We can revisit the suicide pills issue later. Who's that knocking now?"

It was Olivia, with Bernard.

"I'm sorry, Olivia, we're not vets, we can't do anything with a dog."

"Please, Samira. He saved my life. It's just that his haunches keep hurting him. I can't live without Bernard."

"Just a minute Olivia. Bring him in the front."

"No, Samira, we are not..."

"Anjum, she's had a dreadful trauma. The animal provides her psychological comfort over and above what any medications could even approach. You can have a row, but I'm going to do what I can. Frankly, I suspect it's just a sprain, because he overdid it finding and then protecting her."

Not for the first time, Anjum gave way to Samira. He noted that now both death and the dinner would have to wait.

"Samira, it's been a week now, we've been cooking chicken and rice for the dog while we eat tinned fish. The animal is no longer in pain and his back legs have responded very well to the chondroitin tablets, topical ointments and massage, but I am not massaging that creature's haunches any more. It's time he went back."

The truth was that Samira had found herself getting very fond of Bernard.

Returning him heralded her new hope in life...helping children and pets.

Death would definitely have to wait. There was work to be done.

Chapter 4.

RATIONING AND THE BLACK MARKET

"Anjum, what about that special meal you were going to prepare?"

"Forget it. The grocer, the deli, the chain mart, all have virtually nothing. Marjorie from the butcher's told me there's to be some Government address later today. We'd better watch it. Meanwhile 'll rustle something up with the garden herbs, tinned tuna and some rice. And I'll put the news on."

Like everyone else, being used to having anything they wanted on tap 24/7, they had not taken any precautionary measures in case of shortages.

"This is the Prime Minister. You should by now all have received your Government emergency package. The evacuation passes are now starting to roll out and those who are entitled to passes will be receiving them shortly. When you receive your passes, please be sure to queue at the time and place notified in the top left-hand box. Failure to arrive by the appointed time will prevent your evacuation to safety. With so large a number of people to manage and limited resources we really do not have a margin for error.

In the meantime the Government has now taken charge of food supplies. We have begun issuing food parcels, and will continue so to do until the evacuation is complete. These will be distributed at regular intervals to local centres in each town and village, where they can be collected, the operation being administered by the Army. Instructions about your local centres and distribution times are being published on the internet and in the press and distributed to households. You will receive mobile alerts. The government has taken steps to ensure the internet remains running for as long as practically possible, although glitches are inevitable.

I want to thank the stoical and co-operative spirit being shown by the British people at this time. I also salute the admirable work of the armed forces and the police, and the thousands of volunteers who have been and still are assisting in this massive task.

Thank you."

"Anjum, I have received a very odd text, read this."

"It has come to our attention that you do not have settled status and are not entitled to a pass. However, for a moderate fee, my organisation can provide a useable pass."

"It's a fraudster, Samera. I've heard rumblings of a black market in fake passes, rife apparently, causing havoc at the ports. I'll hook him in and we can send notification to the Home Office. Give me your phone."

"I will need your name and details before parting with any money. And what assurances can you give as to the provenance and standard of these passes. From the sound of it they're not legal."

"Just call me Frank. Let's just say 'legal' is a fluid term these days, with rapists, murderers and all sorts running free. My organisation is just providing a service if you like. We have Home Office insiders on board, the passes are from a valid blueprint, and we have had some very happy customers."

"Frank, I want the pass first before money changes hands, and I need to know how much?"

Anjum kept the conversation going until he was satisfied he had sufficient information to nail Frank.

At the sixth attempt the Home Office answered. "I understand and am grateful for the information, thank you," said the officer to who he eventually spoke. "Our problem is staffing, investigations are all on hold. But can you give me some information about yourself and the recipient of the text?" Anjum felt an ironic sense of normality, Home Office bureaucracy was somehow perversely reassuring, it was what he was used to. He was beginning to wish he hadn't stuck his nose in, when the officer finally took him back off 'hold.' "I see you are both Doctors. As such you are both entitled to passes. It's one of the special categories where there is a significant shortage, you will shortly be alerted as to when and where you can collect your valid passes."

Before Anjum could reply she hung up.

Bernard padded in, having just caught some wild animal , obviously devoured with gusto. His muzzle was dripping with fresh blood. Olivia had finally got her appetite back, only that the family's food supply was now meagre. As they sat slowly savouring a box of cornflakes and a tin of baked beans, carefully divided by Maria, Jeremy received a mobile alert. 'There has been an over-estimate of eggs, beef and bread, we can distribute this to you at your convenience, please ring the number below.' Without thinking Jeremy replied eagerly.

"Thank you, your order has been placed, delivery will be shortly after receipt of £300."

"You have to be joking!"

"Food is gold dust now, mate. You can't eat money. Supplies are hard. "Do you want your family to go hungry?"

Jeremy swallowed his principles, buried his conscience, and completed his business with the black marketeer.

As the Ramsay family tucked into a hearty meal, they heard the latest newsflash. "Breaking news. A gang of thieves successfully broke into a government food supply pod in the town of Waybrook, taking everything there, including baby milk. It will take over 24 hours to restock."

The family sat in silence for some time, then Olivia followed up on the story.

"People from the neighbouring towns of Warlock and Temple have shared their own rations with the inhabitants of Waybrook. We rejoice in the spirit of compassion and humanity displayed."

Chapter 5

CHAOS

The PM was in a Cabinet meeting when the Commissioner of the Metropolitan Police was ushered in.

"What's the meaning of this Ivan?"

"Apologies, Prime Minister, but this can't wait. There's chaos at the ports. There are twice as many people turning up as there are passes issued. And more food supplies have been plundered. Organised crime is behind it. We can't contain the situation much longer, and people are still flooding in. Those bloody fake passes are good, and we need the technical equipment to check and verify them."

"All right, Ivan. Get Colonel Bruce to assist. These are your instructions. Makeshift tents and basic facilities are to be erected around the ports' perimeters. The Army will deliver whatever equipment you need. You'll have to check those passes. It will cause serious delays, but there's no choice."

"What do we do with all the people with fakes? The prisons can't be manned, and even if they could, people put in there would all die. Everything and everyone in the country is on the move."

"Don't worry about that Ivan. I will speak to Bruce. Just segregate them."

As the Commissioner left, feeling rather unsettled with his remit, Colonel Bruce was summoned for private talks with the PM. When he arrived, the PM poured 2 large whiskies and brought out the Cuban cigars. With both men fortified they began their talks. They were on first-name terms.

"James, I have collated what I can. It's urgent. We are talking about hundreds of thousands of fakes. The ships can't sail, violence is breaking out and it's escalating as we speak. It's not possible to detain that many people in different parts of the country, nor to transport them all back to their homes."

The PM felt sick. He had spent his life pursuing justice, fairness and compassion, yet here he was. He knew what was coming. He had invited it.

"James, I propose that the ships are guarded by the Army while the passes are scrutinised. Given the numbers involved we cannot simply hold the position if they start to riot. We need power to shoot if necessary. Bear in mind that suggestions of shooting but not to kill are irrelevant, because there is no realistic prospect of medical help for those who are injured, who will therefore probably suffer a slow death instead of a quick one. The shock should restore order for sufficient time to verify the passes. The army will confiscate all false passes, and detain their holders until the ships have sailed, by force if necessary."

"Vincent, you're asking me effectively to order daylight murder. Those without passes may never get home. They will certainly die if not evacuated, or stopped first, and God knows how many will die in trying to re-establish order at the ports. You will say that the end justifies the means, but if we lose everything which makes this country just and free, and we lose every ounce of compassion for our fellow men we lose humanity. I ask you, what are you saying here?"

"James, I'd say you have a maximum of around 4 hours. Consult your Cabinet, and I suggest you access your Computer Bod. It's the best Artificial Intelligence in the world. I know it's awaiting ethics approval, but in a few hours that will all be obsolete."

James gulped down a couple of aspirin, washed down with antacid. His whole mind, body and spirit were in turmoil. He was not a dictator, but... He knew his Cabinet would be split on this, and it was. The majority did, however, agree to refer the issue to the Computer Bod, knowing the answer it would give.

Programme starting in 60 Seconds...

Ships, various, multiple trips, maximum capacity within time frame, 25 million passengers

Small boats, various, limited trips, maximum capacity within time frame, 1 million passengers

Legitimate passes to be issued, 26 million

No legitimate passes for 40 million people

Illegitimate passes in circulation, estimated, 20 million

Chance of survival if not evacuated within 1 month, 20%

Chance of survival if not evacuated within 6 months, nil

Estimated casualties from use of arms successfully maintaining order at ports, up to 8 million. NB: these will predominantly be people who would not be entitled to evacuation and who would therefore not survive in any event

Estimated casualties if rioting prevents any sailing and no-one can be evacuated, 26 million.

Estimated casualties if sailings delayed, with consequent reduced number of possible trips, 5 million per week. NB: these will be people entitled to evacuation and who would otherwise have survived.

Recommended course of action -unrestricted use of arms to maintain order at ports and enable evacuation of those entitled.

Chapter 6

THE MINDSET

The Ramsays received their collection alert for their passes that morning, and the family, save for Olivia, were in good spirits until, huddled around Bernard, they started listening to the news.

"This is the BBC News, brought to you by Vanessa Norton. There has been massive rioting at many of the evacuation ports, where people without passes, or with false passes, have tried to storm the ships. The Army has been able to contain the disorder and enable those so entitled to board, as the evacuation starts to get under way. This has necessitated abundant use of weaponry. Casualties are unknown at this time but are estimated to be in the hundreds of thousands, overwhelmingly among the rioters. The Government has stressed that it is imperative to ensure an orderly, fair and just evacuation of those who can be saved. The alternative is that no-one will be. The younger generations must have priority. The Pass system must be observed. Anyone without a pass, or with a false pass, will be detained, or worse. Under no circumstances will such people be able to board a ship. These measures are for the preservation of humanity. Unless order is maintained chaos will result and all chance of evacuation to a safe destination will be gone."

Jeremy grabbed the last beer. He needed something to bolster his mindset. He had to be positive, and ready for the family onset.

"Maria, by the time we get there this trouble will be sorted."

"Dad?"

"Yes, Nicholas?"

"Will we be shot? By mistake, I mean. Will our passes be stolen?"

"No, don't be silly, Bernard will protect us."

Jeremy took a deep breath. "Olivia, darling, there's not enough room for people, never mind dogs."

"I'm not going without Bernard. I'm not leaving him to die."

"He won't die. I have made arrangements for him."

"What arrangements, Mum?"

"Anjum and Samira will look after him for us."

"Don't be silly. What happens when they get passes? And if they don't, they'll all die. I don't want to live in this new world where people and animals don't matter. Survival of the nastiest? Life isn't worth living anymore, there's no joy, it's all fear, I'm so tired of being frightened and hurt, facing the unknown. At least I know where I am in my dark tunnel"

Jeremy and Maria felt helpless, they had no idea how to console this stranger who was once their lively bright daughter, and they were acutely aware that time was running out. Jeremy tried; "Olivia, it's so hard for everyone, but we have to just get on with it, be stoical." That made things far worse.

Olivia was becoming so hysterical that Maria felt obliged to rush next door.

"Samira, I'm sorry, but Olivia is hyperventilating, she needs help, something to calm her down."

"Anjum, do we still have some Valium in the medical box?"

"Here you are."

Samira's warm, calm presence stabilised Olivia, whom she held tightly as Olivia's tears poured out, soaking Samira's dress. She took her pills and remained in Samira's embrace, with Bernard lying across their feet. An hour or so passed before Anjum appeared.

"Olivia, you must listen to me. Right now, things are bad. But all this will pass. One day you will wake up to a new world, a world where love, compassion and co-operation will rule. Greed and excess have failed and people will learn that. Everything is a cyclical continuum. We are all just atoms and all part of the greater cosmos. There is goodness in most of us and with nurturing it will reign. Bernard will always be with you in your heart. His unconditional love cannot be taken from you.

But now your family and your life must be paramount. You know that. You must be brave for yourself, for them, for us, for humanity. You do not have the time or luxury to grieve. You must prepare to go."

"But what if your passes come? What if they don't? What if..."

"Olivia, no-one can predict the future. The probabilities look bleak, but we cannot know, it is beyond us, we must accept that. We can only hope for the best, but we cannot answer for the outcome of all eventualities. Do not ask 'What if...', accept what will be, however hard, because that is all you can do."

A few hours later the Ramsays set out for Portsmouth, to board the cruise liner Eagle. Fortunately, the rioting there had substantially abated and they were able to settle down on board, like many others, in shock and silence.

"Where are you going Olivia?"

"Just give me some space Mum, please."

She wandered around, looking at all the frightened faces, ending up in the children's area, she saw Emily and a few social workers trying desperately to placate a large number of children, they were all at least alert, except for one little girl, sitting slightly apart, she appeared drowsy, but when Olivia moved closer, she saw the deep mental pain and suffering in her big brown eyes, no tears, too deeply hurt, no Mum and Dad, just strangers. For a moment, Olivia forgot her own troubles, overwhelmed with empathy for this poor little thing who could barely be more than 5 years or so.

"Can I sit next to you? My name is Olivia." The little girl shrugged. Silence.

"Can I tell you a story?" Another shrug. Olivia remembered how she loved her Mum reading Kipling's Just So stories, and could see a copy there. She began with 'The Elephant's Child'. At the end she asked "another one?"

This time there was a "Yes please", not a shrug. She read the 'The Beginning of the Armadillos' and then "How the Whale got his Throat", by which time the little girl was smiling, asking for more stories and saying "my name is Linda." Olivia glanced up at the group, Emily was beaming at her, and many of the younger children had been listening. "You have them spellbound", Emily smiled. "Can you help us look after them, you seem to have a gift". Olivia felt happy for the first time in many months, she could help, make a difference, there was something bigger outside herself. "Of course, I'd love to."

As the ship set sail a message came over the tannoy. "This is Captain Victor, I have to tell you that a child has fallen overboard. We are attempting to rescue her. Please remain where you are. I understand that you may wish to help, but please do not impede my crew during this rescue. I will keep you updated."

Samira and Anjum were finally alone with their thoughts. They were expecting Bernard to come downstairs for his diner.

"Anjum, I can't find the dog. I thought he was upstairs. He could have been missing for hours, oh my God!"

47

"Don't panic, that's not like you. He'll be around somewhere. He's probably hunting for his own dinner, Maria said he does that now."

Back on the Eagle there was a kind of universal anxiety over the little girl, Philippa – her name had become widely known almost instantly – with everyone willing for her to be saved. Despite the tannoy most were on deck or at windows, looking hard and long.

Captain Victor called to the First Mate. "Leslie, what's that creature? It's got a child on its back. What the hell?"

"Captain, it's one of those rescue dogs. A Newfoundland. And it's rescued Philippa."

As Philippa and Bernard were lifted to safety there were cries of relief, applause, laughter. The human spirit was triumphant.

"Captain...isn't it contrary to our orders to have a dog on board?"

"Yes. Unless the alternative is a mutiny and anarchy on board."

"Oh, it would be, Captain, it would be."

Samira and Anjum sat in silence for some time, both thinking the same. It was Samira who broke the silence. "I think it's time now Anjum to revisit that Government-issue pill package. We'll notify the Home Office so someone else can utilise our passes, if they get round to issuing them."

"I too am ready. I had thought, like you, maybe we could be of use, but I cannot fight this grief, even with the bottle."

Samira smiled. "I wonder what lies beyond?"

"Come now, Samira, you know very well, we are no more than our thoughts and actions."

"Maybe, Anjum, maybe our consciousness somehow remains. Even neuroscience tells us the consciousness is the last thing to go and does linger. Do you think we would meet the consciousnesses of our loved ones?"

"Samira, the consciousness disperses back into the cosmos. Our loved ones are with us in our minds, our hearts, our memories. We may pass on those thoughts, actions and memories, so in a way they do live on. So too, by our actions we can teach love and compassion. I doubt there is more."

"But people believe...billions of them."

"Of course, Samira, it gives some cohesion to life and society. These beliefs give meaning and comfort to people. But remember the power of the collective consciousness. That, coupled with a natural tendency to follow traditions and contemporary norms and societal behaviour...and more...maybe to fill a void in an otherwise lonely soul...who knows? What we do know is that our bodies are just water and bacteria, our minds and consciousness a multitude of atoms; rather like a computer with artificial intelligence."

"Well, Anjum, we have done what we can. I think we can say our thoughts and actions have helped other people."

Not for the first time, Samira and Anjum were ready to take their pills in peace and acceptance when there was a loud banging on the door.

"We're rather busy here right now."

"Please, Anjum, you must help. It's Veronica, from the Mansions. We are coming round with Andrew."

Veronica and Tristram had worked hard all their lives in property development. They had left natural childbirth too late, but when Veronica was in her late 50s a private hospital had assisted with *in-vitro* fertilization of her previously frozen eggs, resulting in a successful pregnancy. Andrew, now 14 years old, was their pride and joy.

"Andrew knows and trusts you both, he's so frightened and confused, and we are simply helpless. We are too old to qualify for passes. We have confirmed, his ship serves this locality, you'll be on the same one, please."

As providence would have it, they received their mobile alert for their own passes. It would be feasible.

"Just give us a moment Veronica"

"Anjum..."

"Yes, I know, we'll help. Fortune has other plans for us...wants us alive. I'll make sure Veronica doesn't overpack, while you have a chat with Andrew."

"I'm on it Samera."

Chapter 7

UNCHARTED WATERS

The Prime Minister had called an urgent Cabinet meeting. The Chief Whip kicked off.

"The latest intelligence, matching the news from Reuters is that the Russians have begun a mass exodus to the north. They should be in time to do this, but the countries to the south, Armenia, Georgia, Turkmenistan, Kazakhstan and others, were all refused refugee status by the Russians and are only now able to start moving north as the Russians vacate ahead of them. Their chances of survival are, in the circumstances, minimal. The Russians also refused access to Siberia to the Chinese and Japanese, and the borders are being guarded by the Red Army. Looking west, Canada has restricted entry to only 10% of the population of the US and serious fighting has broken out along parts of the border."

The PM took over.

"We have the same problem. I have spoken to the various Nordic leaders, in Norway, Sweden, Denmark, Iceland and Greenland. Their problem is that they cannot cope with all the potential refugees from Western Europe – us, France, Belgium, Holland and Germany. They have given us a quota. They will take, between them, 15% of the UK refugees. They say their infrastructure, food supplies, water and shelter, cannot cope with anymore."

The questions from the Cabinet went on and on. The most pertinent was from Victor Myers.

"Prime Minister, we know that a significant number of our ships are armed. If dialogue fails, will we have a declaration of war?"

"No, Victor, no declaration. Up to now this has been strictly 'need to know' but probably you now need to know. We have the ultimate threat. One of our Trident submarines is approaching Nordic waters even as we speak."

"Christ, Prime Minister, even the Russians aren't playing that game! Surely..."

There was serious opposition to this suggestion. The Cabinet did not want to be responsible for this. There were suggestions that the Prime Minister was losing it. The debate, or rather row, went on and on. Eventually there was agreement that if the threat failed to achieve its purpose they would not carry it out.

Chapter 8

THE CALM BEFORE THE STORM

The passengers on the Eagle were blissfully ignorant of all this. They expected to be welcomed, with compassion. Olivia and Nicholas had found a string of admirers and were relishing the attention received, courtesy of Bernard. Jeremy and Maria had found some kind of equilibrium. They were proud that their children had, albeit by default, taken on a kind of leadership role, organizing games, singing and play acting. The mood resembled an adventure.

"You know, Jeremy" Maria smiled "all that rubbish we used to think of as being so worrying; the mortgage, the vet's bills, redecorating, well, it's all bollocks."

Jeremy laughed. "So true. I remember how devastated I was when my bloody boss kept trying to make me sack some of my team. He felt I could take on 4 people's work and blithely put 4 families out on the street in the process. He was so coercive. God knows how many sleepless nights I had thanks to that nutter. And it never was resolved."

"You know, Jeremy, in some peculiar way I actually feel free now. If it wasn't for the terrible devastation of parts of the world, and loss of life on an apocalyptic scale, I'd be okay."

"I will always have regrets, like everyone. We should have demanded that the governments took action earlier. All this carnage was avoidable."

"That's the point Jeremy. Like I was saying, everyone was so tied up with their own worries, they blithely assumed that the world leaders would do something. In fact, they did. Global quota agreements were reached, even though some countries only did so on threat of invasion, it's just that it was too little too late."

"But we all knew, at least in the West. The scientists were leaking facts all over the place. Stage 3 tipping was foretold. We had time, we should have joined a collective, worldwide, we had the net, to put out the people's unified voice. But what did we do? We fretted over which colour to paint the sitting room!"

The leaders of the Nordic countries were having a crisis meeting. Incoming data revealed a mass UK migration heading their way, millions over their agreed quota. The consensus was that there would be devastation and a breakdown of civilisation resulting from an immediate population overrun without sufficient infrastructure, space, food or water.

Various options were thrown around; mobilising their armies, using landmines, arming civilians. Their overwhelming concern was to protect their own populations.

Samira, Anjum and Andrew were on the Noble. Samira was wishing she had studied psychiatry to a higher level. It was a hard task trying to explain to a very confused teenager why and how the world went mad.

"If I can understand I'll be okay, but my head is bursting."

"It's okay, Andrew, you can talk to us."

"When I was on holiday in Spain we had to evacuate because of fires. That was three years ago. Mum said the Government was heeding the calls of scientists. She said that the global consortium was enacting worldwide quotas."

"Yes, that is true. But some countries were unable or unwilling to follow. Other countries felt that they alone could not halt global warming, and so they were not prepared substantially to alter their people's way of life. It's not simple. There was a fear about going to war with non-consenting countries, places where we had been allies for hundreds of years. Wars would have been immediate, global warming was not considered so."

"But Samira, it was all over the news, the summer of 2033, with fires all over Europe, Africa almost wiped out and the scientists screaming all over the media that level 2 tipping, sliding quickly towards level 3, was imminent, and that at level 4 all life would be extinct."

Anjum intervened. "He should know the reality, there's no point humouring him. Look, Andrew, some philosophies will tell you that happiness is born from within, that love, compassion, moderation, being in tune with nature, is the key to fulfilment, that excess brings only harm. Sadly, such a philosophy does not make good business sense, so advertising media and corporate giants were in unison to persuade us to want, want, want. This encourages greed, envy anger and ultimately over-consumption. It all snowballs, becomes endemic, like an infection. From this is born so-called free enterprise. Call it progress, call it success, it becomes the new religion."

Andrew fell silent, processing this avalanche of new ideas.

"So if we shared stuff, just took from nature what we needed...then why did Mum and Dad keep working to buy more and more stuff. Why keep developing, concreting over green fields? They were bad."

"No, no, they were as much victims as everyone else. When society rests on the notion that happiness and success are born of external factors that is how people will turn out. If your mum and dad had been brought up in a society where sharing, compassion and moderation were placed on a pedestal, instead of wealth and power, then a different mindset would be born."

"So what you are saying is that people refused to give up their way of life and pretended nothing was wrong, and couldn't fight other similar societies."

"Not all people. Many lived simple and fulfilling lives without plundering resources. But ultimately, yes"

"So what now?"

"Often, out of terrible tragedy and suffering there can be a societal transformation. People are forced to see the ultimate reality, what actually matters. Over time a profound compassion begins to grow. It grows so strong that the seeds of greed wither. This compassion spreads within an individual and among people causing a connective consciousness. This empowers a community, society, country, world even, to live in harmony with the environment and ultimately the cosmos. It yields the deepest understanding that people, animals, nature are all connected. Harm one, you harm them all. That is what happened, now we need to address that."

Andrew had been given enough food for thought. He heard singing and laughter. He followed the songs until he found a group of younger children, where he made himself useful playing with and supervising them

and felt surprisingly uplifted by doing so.

Chapter 9

FOR THE GREATER GOOD

The Deputy Prime Minister, Victoria Fortescue, had just said her goodbyes to her family. She felt heartbroken, yet relieved that they would be safe. Now she was tasked with combatting Cuthbertson's strategies. She summoned his personal private secretary, Henry Baines.

"Tell me straight, Henry. I've heard dreadful rumours about Cuthbertson, please level with me."

"It's not good, Victoria. He has barely slept for months. He's becoming compulsive and quick to anger. He's been living on Turkish coffee, whisky, junk food and uppers."

"What uppers."

"Regular coke."

"What's his latest agenda?"

"The nuclear threat will not be just that if backed against a wall. There is no doubt his mind is disturbed, but he has a number of loyal contemporaries. I cannot get the psychiatrists to section him, not least because all medical facilities are now evacuating. He gets round the remaining medics by stealth – temporarily cuts out the uppers and reminds them that, given the enormity of the crisis, stressful behaviour is normal. Of course, they have no idea of his plans, like many, even high-ranking members. Those details are all classified.

"I need a meet with the PM. Can you arrange that?"

"He won't see anyone at the moment."

The Prime Minister was obsessively going over the evacuation progress data, over and over, when Victoria barged in.

"I'm not seeing anyone. Get out."

Victoria produced a large bottle of vintage whisky, opened but still nearly full.

"Can't drink all this by myself, can I? I've got a couple of glasses."

Victoria had been surreptitiously pouring hers into the Prime minister's large palmetto plant. The Prime Minister soon succumbed to the effects of whisky laced with narcotics. It took much longer for the palmetto.

News of the Prime Minister's demise travelled fast. There was no time, or personnel, for post-mortems or investigations. Victoria called a Cabinet meeting. With unanimous support she contacted the leaders of the Nordic countries.

Chapter 11

REASON

"The United Kingdom apologises unreservedly for its conduct thus far. Unfortunately, a large number of our ships have already sailed; only a small number of unchartered vessels remain in port. We understand the problems with infrastructure and accordingly only the agreed quota of passengers will disembark when the ships dock. All other passengers will remain on board their ships."

The leaders of the Nordic countries acknowledged that the crisis had eased. Dealing with a leader whose responses were sane was a considerable comfort, and they hoped that, if they were not overwhelmed at the outset, more accommodations might be possible. Their discussions began.

"Look, we could have been the refugees" said Kirsten Haraldsdottir, Prime Minister of Iceland. "As it is, our countries are now like Southern Europe used to be, warm, fertile and flourishing, but if we'd had an ice age we'd be the poor sods knocking on someone else's door."

"Well," replied Greta Lundqvist, the Norwegian leader "looking at how the UK Government used to treat their refugees, I'm not sure they'd have been opening doors – more like shoving us down into the cellar and shutting the door. Remember returns to unsafe countries, wave machines and forced deportations?"

"Well, we must be civilised" said Sweden's Thor Johanssen, "we adhere to humanitarian conventions. Without entrenched compassion we would lose the essence of humanity, and without that we are just empty shells." They talked on for some time, now more optimistic than before.

Andrew asked Anjum, after the Noble had reached port, why they were not disembarking. Then there was an announcement from the Captain.

"There is a delay over disembarkation as a result of administrative issues. I understand that steps are being taken to resolve them, but it may take a little time. In the meantime, please remain calm and carry on as before. There is no cause to be alarmed about this. We have supplies aboard for a month, longer if we institute rationing. I shall keep you informed as the situation develops."

People were shocked and disappointed but, fortunately, they did not get angry. They were stoical. Death had become the norm and fear had burned out within their psyche. They were worn down, confused, and as the days went by, further reductions in rations took their toll. Still they clung to hope.

Olivia had been searching for Linda, at last she found her, curled up in a corner. "Are we going to die Olivia?" It was indeed a paradox, for months Olivia had wanted just that, but now she wanted so much to survive, she looked at Linda, seeing deep into her little soul, a sensitive little girl whom she determined to help and comfort. "Of course not, there's just a few problems organising everyone's accommodation, that's all. Here you are, have this." Linda was starving, demolishing an extra ration. Physically Olivia was hungry, but mentally she was full with compassion, she'd manage on that for a while. Only Bernard could boast a full stomach, his diet being greatly augmented by rattus rattus. The one thing they all still had was, ironically, the greatest – their human spirit.

Chapter 12

COMPASSION

One month later, the excess refugees remained aboard ship. Word had got out that their supplies were dwindling. Local people, little by little, started sharing their own limited rations, delivering parcels to the ships by dinghy. Bernard was earning his keep by helping to transport stuff, and in the process becoming well-known in the area.

The news of this developing aid spread fast. It was greatly helped by a news story, initially in the local paper but rapidly spreading across Scandinavia. The pictures showed a little Norwegian girl who had been washed out to sea by a wave, being rescued and brought safely to shore by a large Newfoundland dog "from the English ship" and reunited with her parents.

It was a matter of time before the remaining refugees were gradually, but in increasing numbers embraced, welcomed and integrated. It happened as much by local initiative as by any decisions from the governments, but it happened. Everyone, locals and refugees, worked together to grow food, a process made much easier by the change in the Scandinavian climate, and to build shelters and develop the resources of the areas where they were settling. The refugees had not come entirely empty-handed. Most of the larger vessels had brought seeds and fertilisers as well as their human cargoes, and a variety of other useful building and other materials, all of which was very valuable. Individuals and communities realized that by working together and sharing what they had they could make this work. Physically, everyone was always a bit hungry and rather tired, but it did not matter. Mentally they were at peace with themselves.

Chapter 13

WHY?

Andrew was talking to his youth group about the course of recent events. He told them that his friend Anjum had predicted the outcome. He quoted "out of terrible suffering there can be a societal transformation...over time compassion grows...and the seeds of greed wither."

"But Andrew..."

"Yes, James?"

"Why did we need a catastrophe to make people be kind? If everyone were like we are now we would not have had this suffering. People would have lived like we do now, but with more of everything. I don't understand."

Andrew remembered Anjum's words and really understood them now.

"When society encourages the belief that happiness rests on external factors, then we become slaves to that mantra. Conversely, when the accepted norm is that true happiness can only grow from within a soul fertile in love and compassion, and that is one's goal to achieve, we have finally reached the point where we can call ourselves truly human."

Andrew realized that the members of the youth group were smiling at him, and he felt a deep sense of contentment.

Some months had passed. One day there was a dramatic statement from the Norwegian Prime Minister.

"Over the recent past the scientific community has been closely monitoring the changes to the earth's climate. When Level 3 tipping was reached it produced the catastrophic changes we have lived through, with massive loss of life and an enforced simplification of the lifestyles of those of us who survived. It now appears that this has meant that the tipping point did not prove irreversible. The consensus is that the earth has now tipped back past Level 3 and there are signs that we are reverting to Level 2. With the lifestyles we now lead and the moderate consumption of resources they involve it is hoped that another 5 years should see a further, dramatic cooling of the earth."

A smile appeared on her face. "This may be bad news for the olive trees which are now growing in Norway, but it is wonderful news for humanity."

She concluded, more sombrely "Thursday 1st March has been designated Remembrance Day. On that day we will mourn the billions of people who died, needlessly, because we didn't know how to share, or worse, because we did know what had to be done but lacked the will to do it, because we chose greed, not moderation and sustainability. We must never make that mistake again."

Printed in Great Britain
by Amazon